THE TANTRA
OF
CHIMERA

A collection of cyber-erotica

by Zoë Duff

Second Edition – Paperback Edition

ISBN 978-0-9813065-0-6

Filidh Publishing – A division of Lesley Innovations Business-Cooperative

Victoria, BC, Canada

First Edition – Hand-bound Bedside Edition

ISBN 0-9732770-0-9

Lesley Innovations (Filidh Publishing Division),

Victoria, BC

Hand-bound by TH0SE GREAT LITTLE B00KS, Victoria, BC

Dedicated to:

Crashed, Allante, Silver Knight, Southern Cat, Cathie and especially Big Brown Eyes.

Every woman should have

such a fan club!

<u>Collected for your enjoyment…</u>

Song of the Night - poetry

- A Bedtime Story - a ghostly visitor
- Sharing Dawn - a couple finds a hot bi babe
- Now that's a PowerPoint presentation - some play time on the job
- A Good Man is well trained - a Mistress and her slave
- A Harbour Boardwalk stroll - outdoor escapades along the waterway
- The Cat - an adventure in shapeshifting
- Something kind of special - full moon, lunar eclipse and the beach
- Seek the Heart of a Rowan - a Samurai Warrior & a Celtic Witch
- The Vacation - International internet friends meet
- Diplomatic Relations – two couples wait out a snowstorm
- Exhibiting Restraint - a strict diet pays off in oh so many ways
- Flight of Fantasy - mile high club threesome
- Under the Skull and Crossbones – A pirate Captain & her crew

A Winter Eve - poetry

SONG 0F THE NIGHT

Shadow of the evening fall soft upon my bed,

Wherein I lay awaiting my lover or his stead.

Flowing hair over shoulders of delicacy and grace,

Bated breath and racing pulse cry for his sweet embrace.

My lover comes to me as twilight turns to eve,

We sing the song of loving only lovers can perceive.

Lip to lip we softly speak and silent message share,

Gentle fingers stroke his brow to ease the stress found there.

Too soon my lover leaves, as evening turns to dawn,

And I await the new moon all the while my love is gone.

A Bedtime Story

Weary from a long hard workday, you fall heavily into bed. You set the alarm, shift positions and bedding to get the exact spot that you need to sleep.

You begin to drift off to sleep. Suddenly you become aware of someone lifting up the covers at the end of the bed. You feel someone crawl under the blanket and along your body. Hands caress and undress you. You are alert but sedated by sleepiness and the fact that the attention feels so damn good.

The hands are teasing and caressing you, and your penis is proudly standing at attention. A moan escapes from your throat. A mouth begins to wander over your body, giving special attention to your nipples, scrotum and anus...but no contact with your cock. The teasing is unbearable. Your rod aches to for attention. You lay on your back in the dark, eyes closed. Every muscle in your body focuses on the movement of that mouth.

At last, you feel a very wicked tongue teasing its way up the shaft of your cock...again you moan and say that you need to more. A warm insistent mouth surrounds your throbbing manhood. You gasp at the intense pleasure that it gives you.

The mouth moves up and down on your shaft, faster and faster. The need to shoot your load of delicious cum builds to a frenzy and at last, you cum so hard that you feel weak with the effort. You open your eyes to see the image of my face looking at you from under the covers. I smile. Blow you a kiss, and suddenly I'm gone. The covers drop back into place as though I was never there.

Puzzled, you drift back to sleep thinking that it was perhaps a dream.

Sharing Dawn

I was a bit bored one afternoon, and so I was surfing the online personals. None of the men were interesting, so I wandered over into the Women to Women section. There I found an ad by a man looking for a friend for his wife. He travels a lot on business, and she gets lonesome, but she likes to be intimate with her girlfriends too.

I thought, "Why not?" and sent a response.

I went on with my surfing and Yahoo notified me of an incoming email. It was the man writing back to say that he wanted me to meet his wife. We arranged to bump into each other at a local pub that night.

I arrived a bit early and had a few drinks to get settled. When they came in, I knew them right away from the man's description. He was nice looking and reminded me a bit of you. The wife was a beautiful blonde with a nice firm little body.

She and I chatted and found that we had many interests in common. He was a bit agitated. After a good visit and some drinks, they persuaded me to retire to their home.

Dawn and I were left alone in the living room of their home. The husband had excused himself, as he was tired. Once he was gone, we began to stroke and fondled each other as we undressed. Her touch was wonderful, and her skin was smooth, soft and inviting. Her breasts were small but perky. The nipples jumped to attention, and I was drawn like a fly to a flame.

My mouth hungrily licked and sucked each nipple in turn. Dawn moaned and caressed my breasts. I shifted and let her return the favour. Then I pushed her back onto the sofa and let my tongue explore her tummy and thighs. She moaned softly and sighed with pleasure. I teased her pussy with soft caresses of my fingers while I licked her inner thighs. Her mound thrust at me begging for attention. I ran one finger teasingly along her slit and, with a quick flick at her love button, brought it back down her slit. She gasped and called out for me to eat her.

I repeated the process with my tongue many times until she was writhing in my torment. Then I found her clit and ran my tongue in small circles over and around it. Inserting fingers into her hole, I intensified my licking and nipped occasionally. Her moans were getting louder.

Suddenly I felt a pair of hands stroking my ass and pussy. Then a tongue began to lick my cheeks and the lips of my pussy. The tongue travelled to my clit and fingers began to pump into my hole. With the same motions as I applied to Dawn's very hot crotch, an unseen person was distracting me from my appointed tasks. The tongue between my legs was driving me crazy, and Dawn's moaning and thrusting against my face was very arousing as well. She came with a blast and a shudder.

I leaned back onto my knees to let her up and realized the hubby was there behind me. He continued to caress me from behind, while she lapped at my breasts and belly. She turned onto her back and began to tongue my snatch.

I leaned over her and licked her body all the way to her treasure. I nibbled and teased her, but her tongue was very insistent on my attention. Her husband was licking my anus and cheeks. The sensations altogether were too much, and I felt an orgasm approaching.

He slid his cock into my ass while her fingers pumped my throbbing pussy and her tongue sent me over the edge to a thundering orgasm. I shuddered and groaned, and still, they fucked me until I came several times and was weak in the legs. After quickly cleaning up, we switched positions, and I sucked on his cock, as only I can do. I ran my tongue all over it, up and down the shaft and suckling his balls and teasing his anus. I inserted fingers into his hole just as I took the whole of his rod into my mouth. I could hear him begging for more clearly despite Dawn's pussy being on his face. I grabbed his cock tightly at the base preventing him from shooting his load and made him take more of my torture. Then I sat back as she rode him to their mutual bliss. It was a fun night, and we plan to meet again... the next time I dream this dream...or was it a dream?

Now That's a PowerPoint Presentation

"Hey, there!!!!"
You stop writing on the blackboard in the empty lecture hall and turn to see who called you. There I stand, smiling and wearing nothing but a Mac against another very rainy winter morning. You stride towards me and greet me with kisses. Your hands wander over my body and greet me as well.

"I wonder if I might sit in on your presentation," I say when conversation is possible.

Clients begin to enter the room for your first meeting. I take a seat in the elevated rows and am at such a place that you can see very clearly my lack of panties.

I shift my legs throughout your presentation, and the view is very distracting. After the meeting, I approach you at the lectern. Your next session is moments away. The lectern is portable and set on a large counter with enough space underneath for me. I slip into that space and remove my Mac. I stretch out like a kitten in the sun. Your clients enter the room, and you begin your meeting.

Only you can see me as I begin to caress myself. My hands wander over my breasts and tease the nipples to hardness, and I slide each nipple into my own mouth in turn. My tongue licks and teases the nipples. I moan softly, but only you can hear it. You conduct your presentation and answer a very questioning client while watching me. I note the firm bulge in your pants with amusement.

My hand moves to my fully exposed pussy. It is shaven clean so that you can see it throb in response to my teasing fingers and the moisture glistens in the fluorescent light. My moans increase, as does my passion. You move closer to the lectern to block the view as you can't concentrate and wanting me is making you crazy.

You feel your fly unzip and someone's cool hands release your aching rod from captivity. A very wicked and wiggling tongue torments you further. You are stuttering in your responses to questions. You've lost your place in your notes. A warm and heavenly mouth slides over your cock and pumps with increasing speed, and all you can think of is that mouth. You stop in mid-sentence and moan.

Your co-workers are looking at you with concern and confusion. You recover and finish your pitch. My mouth is pumping wildly on your hardness, and as you grip the edges of the lectern for support, you shoot hot jism in an electrifying response that feels as if it comes from your toes.

The meeting is over. Clients and staff members leave, and you are free for an hour. You crawl under the counter and begin to use your tongue to repay my torture. Your mouth is everywhere at once, and I moan and squirm under your attention. You pull me out from under the counter.

Pushing me up against the blackboard, you hoist me up to thrust your pulsing weapon inside me. I wrap my legs around your waist and my arms around your neck. You bury your face in my nipples and thrust your hardness into me with a blinding fury making me orgasm repeatedly and with force. You pound into me again and again and again.

Chalk, erasers and assorted items fly around the room. The blackboard hinges give on the one side. I am begging for more and more. Your cock is filling and demanding and the more you give me, the more I want. My juices flow warmly down your legs. Finally, you surrender to the pleasure and send your hot seed into my pussy.
We tidy up the room and ourselves and leave the hall.

A Good Man is Well Trained

Hop out of your clothes then, and stretch out on the bed just here. I have these lovely undies for you to wear. A rubbery material - we call it PVC in Canada. It's a kind of a stretchy vinyl that can be very warm. Slide them on. There's a pet. Now lay back on the bed...up a bit higher. That's it!!
I'm going to handcuff you to the headboard, so your arms are spread very wide. There that's fine. Now stretch your legs out towards the foot posters...yes that's it. I'll use these silk ties for your ankles. There, is that too tight? Good. A bit tight is fine, as they'll loosen up a bit in a while.

I'll tie the other ankle in a sec first...roll a bit towards the fastened ankle. Okay, now I have an anal plug for you. It fastens into a little pouch in the back of your undies and slides into your anus just so. How does that feel? It's going to feel more than peculiar, my love. LOL.

Okay, all set there. Let's fasten the other ankle. Very good. Now here's a bit of a surprise for you. A ball gag. Ever had one before? A string fastens over each ear and holds a little ball about the size of a golf ball in your mouth. It muffles your screams.

Will you scream? Oh, I hope so.
I love it when you moan and beg for my hot pussy.

There now the gag is in place.

Now I put a blindfold on you. There, now we're all
set. Nothing you can do but experience what I
choose to do to you. And you have been a very bad
boy...
I remove my clothing and begin by running my
hands all over you and rubbing my skin against
yours. You relax and enjoy the contact.

I have another surprise for you. I pull your undies
down in front and rub oil onto your penis and balls.
It instantly feels warm and tingles. I reach behind
and switch the anal plug on. It begins to vibrate
inside your anus gently. The oil I've used is a
Chinese concoction that causes you to get hard and
stay that way. It feels like a thousand fingers and
tongues caressing you all over your cock and balls.
You are instantly rock hard. Your cock wants to
release...NOW! I tuck it neatly back into the pants,
and they form around it so that I can lick you
through it and you feel my mouth and tongue. The
warmth of the vinyl makes the chemical act more
so, and a thousand fingers move faster. You moan
and fight against your restraints. You can think of

nothing, but you need to fuck me. The anal probe is sending bizarre sensations throughout your body and loosening your control...

I run my tongue all over your body. You never know where it will be next and I suck your cock through the vinyl driving you mad.

Oh...by the way...the chemical doesn't react well with the chemicals in sperm... It will cause a severe chemical burn if you cum. You must not cum. Now you really start fighting the bindings. You think you've hooked up with a complete wacko and are in fact a bit scared. The penis wants to shrivel but can't...the chemical keeps it hard and yearning for me.

You try to hurl verbal abuse at me, but the ball gag is in the way. You are helpless, and you are MINE!

I slide the pants down again and put a condom over your cock. I don't want to get burned, after all. I suck your cock through the condom and your balls ache like you've been kicked. You want to cum desperately.... You want my wet and alluring pussy. You are writhing and bucking against the bindings. Your feet are nearly loosened. I jump on top and ride your hard aching cock. It feels so good. You want to climb inside my pussy and pitch a tent. You want me. You fight your body's need to cum as you are terrified of the chemical burn...but it feels so good. I ride you to the edge of orgasm...then stop and begin again. You think you will lose your mind. Then suddenly you can fight no more and you cum so hard the tip nearly blows off your cock. I dismount. Removing the condom, I wipe you off with a cool cloth and begin to untie your binds.

"What about the chemical burn?" you say.

"Just playing head games with you, darling. I would never

hurt you. But you were a very bad boy. "

Your legs are loose. The pants and probe are gone. I straddle you and remove the blindfold and ball gag.

"Wait until I get my hands on you...you bitch," you say.

"That's Mistress Bitch to you, ass wipe."

I slap your upraised leg. Holding my breasts above your mouth I say:

"Do you need another lesson on how to behave, Slave...or are you ready to please your Mistress?"

A Harbour Boardwalk Stroll

It's a lovely bright morning, very early, and a bit on the cool side. A mist drifts in off the ocean. We walk hand in hand along the harbour walkway. It is quite beautiful. There is a thickly wooded area just ahead. There seems to be no one around.

We slip into the woods and find cement and wooden park bench about 5 feet long. It is surrounded by the growth of the woods now but can be seen from the path if one were to look for it.

We sit on it together and snuggle against the coolness. Through the trees, we can see the water and anyone walking along the path. You are nuzzling my cheek and ear, and my lips find yours. We kiss and out tongues mingle and caress one another. I open your jacket and crawl inside... my hands caressing you and then more urgently undoing my jacket and blouse.

Your mouth finds my throat and breasts. Your fingers tease my nipples through my bra.

I moan and knead your back with my fingers...encouraging you to free my aching breasts. You reach behind me and unclip my bra, then free each nipple in turn. The coolness and freedom make them harden to their fullness, eager for your consideration. Your fingers caress and tease them, and I whisper..." please, baby, please!"

You slowly and deliberately begin to lick one nipple, while teasing the other with your fingers in similar motions. I writhe in delight and torment, trying to be quiet and going crazy with need. Your tongue moves from one nipple to the other and back. The coolness and moisture of your tongue keep them cold and rock hard. Your hand slides under my skirt finds no panties and seeks out my slit. You take one finger and teasingly wiggle it along my slit, just grazing my clit. I can't stand much of that, but you make me endure it, and then you slide off the bench to your knees. You part my legs and give my clit what it wants. I am so hot; I fairly lift off the bench with the orgasm that rips through my body. I want to suck your cock. I HAVE to suck your cock.

You stand before me, and I take your wonderful manhood into my mouth. I lap and lick and suck. You want to bury your shaft in my hole, and so I stand up and go around the back of the bench. I lean forward hanging onto the back, and you slide that pulsing rod of yours into my dripping pussy. I can't help but groan as it enters me. It's so huge and hard. It feels so good.

You thrust slowly driving me completely up a wall. I whisper endearments, I beg, I promise to suck your cock all the way home in the car...anything just PLEASE...pound that stiff rod into me.

You keep the thrust slow and tortuous as you note some folks are walking by. You tell me that I must pull open my jacket and bare my breasts to these people, fondling them...so they may see should they choose to look. I do this as requested.

They walk by, glance our way at birds above us, but don't see us. Another orgasm rips through me, as you knew that being exposed would excite me beyond belief. You pound your cock into me, and I can't control my groaning...It is incredibly good...I want more of your cock inside me.   I want you to fuck me…yes...hard...like that...Oh my God...oh…just as I think I can't bear anymore, You stop.

Pushing me to the ground on my back, you straddle

me and put your cock between my breasts and into my mouth. You make your final thrusts into my face and cum into my mouth. I swallow your wonderful gift and lick you clean. You decide that I deserve to be punished for being such a slutty little girl.

Still straddling me you hold my wrists above my head with one hand, and pull my clothes open and away with other. People are walking by, but the bench blocks any view now. You lick and suck my breasts, and your tongue and hands are all over me. You bind my wrists with your belt. Your fingers work my clit into another frenzy, but you won't let me cum. You straddle me again and ask if I want your cock. I tell you that I do want it ...I MUST have it ...**now**... you say that you will only give it to me if I can throw you off. I begin to struggle to get you off me. You have leverage and strength on your side. I try using my weight, but tire.

"Oh I guess you don't want it badly enough," you say.

Your fingers are in my hole pumping, your thumb teasing my love button. I want you inside me so badly that my pelvis is cramping. I renew my struggle and at last push you off. I straddle your cock and ride you roughly until I find the satisfaction for which I ached. I have to sit facing your feet and to hang onto your bent knees as my hands are still bound. This position is very deep, and your cock gives me great pleasure as it slides into the depth of my hunger. We reach a point of contentment and begin to collect ourselves. We look like we've been mud wrestling. As we slip out of the woods and back onto the path, you say...

"What was that you promised about sucking my cock all the way home?"

The Cat

Gazing into the depths of the well, I see blackness falling silently into the abyss. I fall into the darkness and tumble out at the base of the well into a long tunnel cut into a mountain. There are torches mounted on the walls of the tunnel, and I can see sure footing to walk along it. The light up ahead is brighter, and I find my way to its source. A well-decorated room, lit only by firelight and a few candles, appears at the next bend of the tunnel.

I enter the room, as I am cold now, dressed only in a thin nightgown. The room is comfortable in the warmth of the fire. There is an overstuffed loveseat and armchair huddled by the fireside. A huge mantle decorated with an assortment of collectibles and candles encloses a roaring fire. All around the room are various dressers and tables festooned with a wide array of fruits, cakes, and bottles of drink.

Several arrangements of cut flowers are about the room. There is a thick rug on the floor and mirrored tiles on the ceiling. A huge four poster bed with a canopy of gold and green brocaded fabric overpowers the room. Many pillows cover the bed and nearly cover the throw that appears to be made of fur.

On either side of the bed are small tables on which are placed bottles of oils and a curious display of items often associated with sexual play.

I feel as though I am being watched and turn to see a man sitting in the armchair by the fire. He is perhaps six feet tall and long in the leg. His long delicate fingers stroke his goatee thoughtfully as he watches me.

In an instant he is at my side, gazing down into my eyes. His hair is light brown and curls down past his shoulders. His eyes, blue and intense, hold my gaze, and I cannot tear my eyes away, even as his hands move to undress me. He wears an earring in his left ear and tufts of curly brown hair peeking from the laced neck of his white cotton shirt. His pants and boots are both leather and laced as was common in an older time.

I stand before him shivering in my nakedness with my nightdress crumpled at my ankles. His caresses move me to a relaxed state of being. He picks me up in his arms and carries me to the bed as though I am precious and needing protection. He lays my body across the coverlet and arranges the pillows just so. He resumes his fingertip exploration of my eager body. Waves of pleasure roll over me, and fingers soon transform into a wise and studied tongue, which knows the secrets of my needs and desires.

As my pleasure builds and I writhe under the torment of his tongue, I observe that my flesh is changing and becoming a fine golden fur. I roll onto my belly and up onto my knees and take his hardened manhood into my depths. He mounts me from behind, and his cock feels as though it expands to fill me. We are locked together, and the thrusting seems to go on past my endurance as one crashing orgasm meshes with the next. I glance over my shoulder and see that the man mounting me is covered in a dark fur, his features catlike and his eyes a blazing yellow.

When the coupling is completed, we lick and groom each other and bat playfully with our claws. The fur fades away, and the skin is once more all that can be seen. Soon the playfulness turns to foreplay, and a bottle of oil is selected from the bedside table.

He warms the oil in his hands and then begins to apply it to my back and legs. It tingles warmly and makes me want to be touched. His hands methodically move over my body, and I enjoy the attention. At his prompting, I roll over onto my back, and he massages the front side of me. His hands linger on my nipples and tease my crotch. I reach up and begin to massage his nipples and cock.

He positions himself over me so that he may taste the sweetness of my pussy and offer me a taste of his hardness. I take his cock into my mouth, hungrily licking and lapping. His tongue finds my clitoris and moves in persistent circles over it. I begin to ache with need and suckle his manhood more aggressively. I moan and shudder as the movements of his tongue drive me to the edge and pull me back repeatedly.

Finally, he adjusts his position and thrusts his hard rod deep into me, lifting my legs over his shoulders. As I near climax, I gaze up into his cat face with glowing eyes and caress his human arm and back. My body is dusted with golden fur but otherwise human. I buck and arch my back as I cum. He hangs on and rides me for successive orgasms.

He offers me food and drink. We sit by the fire and make love on the loveseat. The night passes with unending passion.

In the morning, I awake at home in my bed. My nightdress is in shreds on the floor, and my body aches as though I have been riding a horse bareback. One breast has a mark made by sucking and rubbing the teeth. I am alone. I look at the half-empty cup of tea on the bedside table and the tape recorder with its now silent self-hypnosis cassette and wonder how to find my way back to my cat lover.

Something Kind of Special

The alarm rang shrilly in the darkness and her arm appeared from beneath the comforter to silence it. She struggled out of the covers and set about preparing herself. Showered and dressed warmly, she gathered blankets, wallet and keys. Checking her watch, she donned a jacket and slipped quietly out of the apartment willing the children to sleep.

As she exited the building, she saw him approach from near his car that was parked in the lot. He approached her, kissed her softly and guided her to the passenger side of the vehicle. He took the blankets from her and put them in the back seat.

Then he opened her door and tucked her safely into the passenger seat.

They drove for a time through the city, which still slumbered, in the predawn darkness. The excited tension between them was tangible but not strained. They chatted lightly, both deep into their anticipatory thoughts of what was ahead.

Soon enough they arrived at the beachhead as planned. Selecting a reasonably sheltered area, he pulled the car off the roadway and parked in an assigned location. They paused for a minute to take in the full moon's gleam on the water and the pink streaks of dawn on the horizon. Although the full bloom of summer was in effect, it was a cool morning, and the dampness of the dew-covered sand chilled them through the blankets they laid on it. He settled into the nest of blankets and waited while she called upon the moon as her ancestors had for many lifetimes. She turned slowly calling to her the elements of nature and cosmic wisdom of many ages gone by creating a circular space between the worlds to consummate her affections for him.

He drew her into his arms and kissed her tenderly. As the kisses became deeper, he undressed her slowly and deliberately enjoying the feel of her softness and the way her skin responded to the chill of the morning. His mouth followed his fingers and found her nipples hardened with longing.

She moaned and reached to undress him and return the pleasure he had given her. Touching, caressing, kissing, licking and nipping gently with increasing passion, the lovers moved beneath the blankets under the glow of the full moon and the rising of a new day.

As he removed the last of her clothing, an older couple walking their dogs wandered along the beach mere yards from the nested lovers. After they passed, he rose to his knees, the blankets slipping from his body exposing his taut flesh to the Coast Guard vessel moored in the harbour not far off. He pulled the covers away from her teasing that the ship had cameras focused on her. He entered his goddess of the full moon morning with firm resolve.

She bucked and moaned gripping his shoulders with pleasure and at last grabbing his butt cheeks to encourage the depth of his endeavour. They cuddled together and watched the dawn marvelling at the beauty of all around them and listening to the serenade of the seabirds.

After some time, she rolled over onto him and kissed him deeply began to wander down his body seeking tasty parts to lick and nibble. Soon enough his passion soared, and he mounted her from behind as she leaned against the giant driftwood. Her moans and struggling added to his excitement and they were joined once again in ultimate delight.

Too soon the sounds of an awakening city interrupted their reverie, and they gathered up the nest. She called again as in olden days and thanked the goddess for the blessing of love, shared in tribute to the fullness of the moon.

Over coffee, they relived the wonderment of their special moments, and he drove her home to slip in just as the household began to respond to the new day.

Seek the Heart of the Rowan

She came running over the brow of the hill, a flame of hair and a trail of green tartan behind her. Breathless she stumbled, pot over teakettle down the hill and through the heather. Pausing to collect herself; she saw him.

He had seen her viewing him with an open and child-like curiosity that was quite distracting from his morning meditations. He was struck by the bright vibrancy of her hair against the pale fragility of her skin.

An angry mob with farming implements and torches were in pursuit across the vastness of grass and heather. The Samurai watched with amusement and considered that these old men would likely never catch the woman, but the red-faced women might be worthy adversaries.

The woman arrived at his side and sought his help to escape her fate, which was to be a witch burning.

The Samurai swung silently onto the saddle of his horse and seated the woman behind him. She wrapped her arms snuggly around the Obi at his waist, and he rode away with his prize.

After a few miles, they entered a deep wood, and he slowed his horse to a pleasant trot. Speaking over his shoulder, he asked the woman what had caused the townsfolk to wish her such harm. The woman told of a young farmer who made unwanted advances to a poor travelling wise woman. When the farmer's chickens ceased to lay eggs, he blamed her vengeful hexes. She professed to be nothing more than a storyteller and healer of simple ailments.

Now, the Samurai had seen much in his journey, and he doubted that the woman was so inconsequential. He did not, however, feel a malicious energy about her and her field flower scent was most disarming. The warmth of her body against him penetrated his armour in an oddly familiar way.

Ever alert in ways that become instinctual to a warrior of his ilk, he was instantly aware of danger ahead. She felt his tense and smelled a warning from her own travelling experience. The scent of nervous men, long on the road, signalled the presence of highwaymen in the woods.

From the corner of her eye, she caught the glint of steel. In a flash, he was on the ground Katana in one hand, Wazikoshi in the other. Steel clashed, and the men fought with furor. There were four of them fighting the Samurai, and he bested them with the honourable ferocity of his kind. She was pulled from the horse and thrown like a rag doll to the ground. A sweating stench of a man fell upon her and fumbled with her skirts while several others searched the horse's packs. Hurling curses and flailing her limbs, she fought off her attacker in time to see the Samurai slay him as the last man standing.

She threw her arms around his neck and kissed him full on the lips. He, bravest and most feared of his Emperor's warriors, felt his knees buckle and his loins stir.

Resuming their journey, they went deeper into the woods to a place unknown and unwelcome to many. It seemed to him that the forest held its breath and watched them as they travelled. So dark and hushed were their surroundings that it was almost tomblike.

At the thickest part of the wood, when the horse could pass no further, she raised her arms and called out an ancient chant familiar to his ears. The leaves parted revealing a large clearing. They entered on foot, and the animals came forward to nuzzle her in greeting.

A settee was there for him to recline upon while his horse grazed freely. Nearby a table groaned with fruits of every description. She brought him a cup of brass and told him to sip slowly on the steeping broth of herbs within it. She tended to the wounds he had received in his earlier battle, encouraging him to relax and rest. He stretched out on the settee. The warm drink made his head tingle and the aches of long travel ease from his limbs. The woman shifted animal skins to cover him as he began to doze.

The fog of sleep shifted unwillingly, and he suspected that the brew she'd given him was to blame. He rubbed his eyes against the light and gathered his wits. A great blazing bonfire rose up in the centre of the grove. All around the edges of the firelight animals of every manner reclined peacefully.

To the north of the fire, stood the woman clothed only in a hooded robe of animal skins and feathers. In one hand she held a great, carved staff with a huge stone bound to the tip. Her other hand and face were upraised to the heavens. The most beautiful, haunting melody curled from her lips and caressed him with gentle, sweet fingers.

He watched transfixed as she removed the robe and began to dance around the fire. Leaving the staff with her robe, she had taken his sword in her hands, stretching her arms above her head.

Her breasts swung unfettered as her body gyrated in the fire glow. He unconsciously dropped his jaw marvelling at the vision. Her breasts were larger than he'd seen before. The skin shone palely in the flickering light, contrasted by the dark pink fist-sized areolas and nipples hardened to surpass his thumb in length.

The thickness of her waist and fullness of her hips were in perfect balance and created an exotic image to this man so long on the road and so far from the palace geisha.

She anointed the sword, hilt to tip, with oil and placing the sword tip against her throat; she gently grazed the skin to her navel.

Holding the hilt, she passed its carved surface over her skin only pausing to caress her nipples and give attention to the thatch of fair hair between her legs. Taking the crossbar into her mouth and running her tongue along the carvings, she caressed the shaft of the sword.

Suddenly she thrust the sword into the ground at an angle. She lowered herself onto the sword hilt and thrust her hips toward the ground, grinding the hard metal into her moistness. His sword of flesh chose that moment to alert him from his catatonia forcefully, and he leapt to his feet. The sweetness beneath the thatch of fair hair was swallowing his weapon with increasing frenzy. The woman caressed and pinched her nipples while her passions mounted.

This was too much for him, and he strode to the woman's side pushing past the animals and abruptly hitting an unseen wall.

As he watched, unable to approach any closer, the woman's passion and life energy raised a windstorm in the grove. He raised his hands to keep the flying debris from his vision, and when he saw her again, she stood before him dressed again in her robe.

He was speechless with desire for her, yet something at the edge of his memory made him ache for the loss of her love.

She took him by the hand close to the fire, disrobing him while kissing his brow and body. He touched the softness of her skin and tasted the sweetness of her mouth.

She cut strands of hair from each of them and twined them together while chanting under her breath. Taking his smaller Tanto blade, she made a small cut in each one's palm, mixing their blood in a handshake and tying the braid around their wrists. Next, she called into the heavens for the blessings of the moon upon their hearts. She rubbed their blood on the braid and tucked it into a sack of animal skins.

She kissed him deeply as she returned to his arms and as their kisses deepened his hands traversed the vast softness of her body happily.

He felt a peculiar sense of belonging. It was as though he had once long ago been to this moment and place.

He tasted the honey of her flesh, and his hunger was fuelled by the guttural moans that arose from her throat. She writhed and purred as he lapped at the tuft of hair that marked the gate to his paradise at once lost and found again.

She pulled him towards her digging her nails into his back, and his sword of flesh regained its pulsing sheath. Her cries of passion escalated mixing with the moans of pleasure he could no longer suppress. The warmth of her drew such an eruption of power that he felt as if his entire body was inside her. Again and again, the hunger overwhelmed him, and he thrust deeper and deeper into the heat and the need that was his seductress.

He never wearied but found each summit merely a plateau to the next peak. She was an insatiable huntress, and he was her strong young buck eager for the hunt. Much too soon, the birds began their morning greeting, and the animals disappeared from the clearing. He warmed himself by the embers of the fire, and she collected the remnants of her simple ailment cures.

She bade him dig a hole at the base of the largest Rowan tree in the grove, and there he buries the twine of hair in its sack.

Returning to confirm the deed accomplished, he found the clearing deserted but for a scarf of green cloth still bearing the scent of field flowers. A cold morning mist filled the woods but off in the distance he could hear a soft voice whispering....

"Our love 'tis always been and t'will always be, my brave warrior. Listen, and I am ever with you. I sing in the breeze of the Rowan tree."

The Vacation

She waded through the crowded airport to the arrival area. She moved quickly and deftly within the mash of bodies narrowly avoiding collisions with several suitcases. A luggage car wove through the throng dividing it as surely as Moses must have split the waves so long ago.

Arriving at the appointed spot she waited, shifting from one foot to the other, watching intently for a face familiar only from photographs and twisting a homemade cardboard sign in her hands. Suddenly there was that beautiful, sweet face of an angel.

"Marie-Claire! Marie-Claire!" she called out. "Ici! Ici!"

The angel turned and saw her sign, which read "Marie-Claire," in big bold letters, she ran to the waiting woman and flew into her arms. The women exchanged hugs and kisses, all the while chattering greetings.

Gathering together Marie-Claire's goodly supply of luggage, the two women made their way from the airport to the woman's car.

Driving out of the airport, parking the woman remarked in broken French that Marie-Claire was more beautiful than her photos and that she hoped her visit to Canada was worth the trip from France. Marie-Claire replied in perfect but thickly accented English that the woman was also quite beautiful and that this trip had been a dream since they had met on the Internet.

Cruising along the straight of the highway the two women chatted and listened to soft music on the car stereo. The warmth between the women was instantaneous and seemed to be there naturally.

The visitor was shown to her guestroom and given a quick tour of the woman's house. She took a shower and changed from her travelling clothes while the woman prepared a meal for her guest. They sat by the fire on pillows strewn on the floor and ate the meal and drank some wine, which Marie-Claire had brought as a gift for her hostess.

The warmth of the wine and the happiness of new friendships glimmered long after the fire began to fade to embers. As evening turned to morning; they drifted off to sleep snuggled together on the pillows.

Dawn awakened the chorus of birds and the women stirred. As she stirred, her hand brushed against the younger woman's bare breast and sensing the feel of skin under her fingertips, the woman opened her eyes. Marie-Claire was awake and laying next to her. The angel was even more beautiful in her nakedness. The visitor caressed the woman's face affectionately slowly tracing the line of her lips and tip of her tongue. An intense flame of arousal shot through the woman's body and her fingertips returned to the offered breast. The woman caressed and licked Marie-Claire's lithe body slowly and deliberately. Marie-Claire moaned and began to remove the woman's clothing. They kissed deeply, tongues entwining. Marie-Claire tasted the woman's taut nipples, biting her gently.

The two women adjusted positions several times each wishing to please the other and have her full attention. Marie-Claire straddled the woman's head and leaned forward making her face level with the woman's snatch. Marie-Claire licked and teased the woman's clit in mimicry of the aggressive and tormenting tonguing the woman was giving her. Flickers of pleasure went from her pussy up her back numbing her brain. It was so very good. The woman was tenacious, and her tongue would not stop. Waves of orgasm washed over Marie-Claire as she struggled to maintain her focus in the seductive duel. Marie-Claire shuddered violently and slid off the woman, crumpling on the pillows beside her. Arousal spent she dozed and did not notice the woman get up.

A few moments later, the woman returned with a 12-inch dildo. She awoke Marie-Claire's passion again with that untiring tongue and slid the dildo into her juicy wet hole. Marie-Claire writhed and moaned, digging her fingernails into the crown of the woman's head. Her back arched with the force of the orgasm that rocked through her body. This would truly be the best of all vacations.

Diplomatic Relations

Tim ran the last check of the house making sure that all windows and doors were locked. He whistled happily to himself. It would be nice to get away for the weekend. He and Sue were dropping the kids off at their grandparents' home and spending the next few days ice fishing at Corbett Lake. Tim grinned widely. He didn't imagine that he'd be doing much fishing. Time alone with Sue was much too distracting.

Vancouver was deep into the winter rainy season, and they were relieved to see the fog clearing as they drove into Chilliwack. The overcast sky threatened, but the snow line was still quite high. Tim anticipated an enjoyable trip through the mountains along the Coquihalla Highway. Just south of the town of Hope, it began to snow. Sue and Tim's enthusiasm for their trip increased with each mile.

The snowfall increased quite suddenly, but Tim pressed on, as the road was still clear. The higher into the mountains they travelled, the worse the roads got. Sue expressed concern as visibility decreased and Time struggled to control fishtailing of the camper van. Tim knew the road well, but Sue had not travelled in mountain snow before. Aware of her nervousness, Tim had overdone his supplies for his trip. He knew that they could wait out the snow quite comfortably in the camper.

Finally, Tim had to pull to the side of the road and wait for a snowplow, checking the vehicle and determining that it was safe. Sue played with the radio to find road condition alerts and determine the expected length of the delay.

While outside, Tim observed the lights of a vehicle swerving wildly towards him. A gray Mercury Sable came into view, and the driver pulled over to the side of the road just behind Tim's vehicle. Sue appeared at Tim's elbow to tell him that the RCMP had closed the highway and even snow vehicles had been pulled off the road. Fifty centimetres of snow had fallen in the last hour, and there would likely be that much again before long. There would be no snowplows until morning. Night falls abruptly in the mountains, and winter temperatures drop with the light. It was suddenly very dark and very cold.

The driver of the car had approached and introduced himself in the midst of Sue's road conditions update. He was horrified. He and his wife had flown into Vancouver from Dallas, Texas the week prior. They were driving a rented vehicle to Kamloops to attend a wedding. They had never seen snow before and had made no preparations for such weather.

Sue and Tim were quick to offer the hospitality of a warm meal in their camper. Jack went back to the car to relay the invitation to Shirley. During dinner, Tim and Jack talked about the upcoming Superbowl while Sue and Shirley discovered a shared interest in golf.

When Tim went out to check the camper's vents for snow accumulation, he wrapped Shirley in Sue's parka and walked her to the car to get her overnight bag. Jack and Sue cleaned up the supper dishes. Jack was funny and flirted outrageously with Sue. Sue found herself responding in kind. Their bodies brushed against each other repeatedly in the confines of the kitchenette.

Tim had found his eyes wandering to Shirley's prominent cleavage. She was as attractive as Sue but in a different way.

Tim and Shirley returned to the camper shuddering from the cold. Jack and Sue had lowered the table and pulled out the hide-a-bed. Sue laid out several warm blankets and lots of pillows. Jack was choosing videotape to play on the camper's small television system.

"I think all we brought was porno this trip," said Tim, with a sheepish grin.

"That'll warm me up quickly." chirped Shirley, snuggling in beside Sue.

Sue was pushed against Jack wedging him against the side of the van. Tim topped up everyone's coffee with more Brandy and slid onto the bed next to Shirley. The lights of the camper were dimmed. The view of Shirley's breasts and the pressure of her body against his body were equally distracting. Shirley took his hand and placed it on her right breast. Her hard nipple poked at him through her dress. Startled he glanced at Sue to see how deep in the doghouse he was.

Jack was massaging Sue's breasts under her shirt and running his tongue from her earlobe to her collarbone. Sue's eyes were fixed on the group sex scene of the video. Shirley's hand was rubbing his crotch through his jeans.

The movie scenario changed, and Tim collected empty coffee cups. He returned to find three naked people on the bed. As he removed his clothes, he watched Jack and Shirley each suckle his wife's nipples. Sue moaned. Her eyes met his, and she smiled.

Tim thought he'd never seen her so beautiful. Tim alternated his attention between both women's pussies. Teasing and tormenting them with his fingers and tongue. Jack pinched Shirley's nipples, and Sue stroked Jack's cock.

Bodies shuffled, and Jack slid his cock into Sue's mouth. Sue, on her knees, straddled Shirley who licked and lapped Sue's throbbing clit. Tim knelt on the floor and tormented Shirley with his tongue. He licked playfully over every inch of her pussy while his fingers worked there way deeper and deeper into her hole. Shirley bucked and twitched under his attention. Her tongue and fingers worked fanatically on Sue's clit. Sue shuddered and bucked in response and tilted her head just in time for Jack's load to spray into the air.

There was a brief pause in the festivities as the ladies cleaned up and straighten pillows.

Tim, still sporting a firm and demanding erection, was encouraged to stretch out on the bed for his rewards. Jack poured himself more Brandy and watched Sue and Shirley began kissing and licking Tim. They began with his lips and licked down his chest and around his nipples. Their tongues were insistent and moved in tandem. Arriving at his genitals, Sue licked and sucked his testicles one at a time. Shirley gave him an award winning blowjob. Her mouth teased him to the edge and then stopped. Then suddenly was on him again. Tim groaned with the need to release. Sue's tongue found his anus and licked it mercilessly.

Shifting position, Shirley straddled his cock backwards facing his feet. Sue kneeled in front of Shirley alternating her attention between Shirley's clit and Tim's balls. Shirley rode Tim's cock with aching slowness.

Jack came in behind Sue and thrust his cock into her with deep and abrupt strokes. All four lovers moaned with increasing fervour. The thrusts became faster and the moans louder. The van rocked in response to the passion within and the storm without.

Finally, satiated and giggling, the foursome chatted lying naked together. Sue and Jack climbed into the upper bed, and they dozed off in each other's arms. Periodically, throughout the night, the heater would cut out. Awakened by the coolness of the camper, the lovers would snuggle closer. Tim awakened several times to find Shirley sucking the erection inspired by her closeness. He would hear the unmistakable sounds of his wife sucking Jack's cock or her moans as Jack pumped her over and over again.

Tim and Sue had always had an active sex life, but tonight they were both on fire. Tim couldn't believe how quickly he responded to Shirley's constant hunger.

The weather cleared just before dawn and the snowplow passed by making travel possible. It took Jack and Tim an hour to drive the vehicles to the next rest stop. Sue and Shirley travelled in the back of the camper together.

Tim was vaguely aware that the chatting and giggling had died away when he parked in the rest stop parking area. Jack pulled in beside him, and the men checked the vehicles while they waited for the women to emerge.

Finally, puzzled by the delay, Tim knocked on the door and called to Sue. Hearing no response, he unlocked the door and entered the camper with Jack following.

Sue and Shirley were entwined on the bed rapidly tonguing each other and pumping rubber dildos into each other's hole. The frenzy of the activity was overwhelmingly arousing.

Tim and Jack exchanged looks, locked the door and got naked.

Now, ***this*** *is a whopper of a fishing story* thought Tim, with a chuckle.

Exhibiting Restraint

The mist of the happy dreams parted abruptly with the annoying blare of the alarm. She stretched and arose for the day. Rubbing sleep from her eyes, she wandered into the bathroom and began her morning preparations.

She stepped onto the scales and looked down. 120. She stepped off and back onto the scales again. 120.

"Oh, my gawd!" she said. "Honey, I did it! Brad! Come quickly! Come and see!"

An alarmed man shrouded in sleep stumbled in the bathroom door.

"What's wrong?!" He said

"I did it! I'm down to 120 pounds!"

"Oh, that's wonderful, baby! I'm so proud of you!" he said, hugging and kissing her.

Rebecca felt lighter and taller all day. Several people from their circle of friends called to congratulate her that evening. Brad said that they were planning a special celebration for that weekend. Rebecca had followed a strict diet and exercise program for just over a year. Rebecca and Brad enjoyed a lifestyle that included nudism and swinging. Rebecca, although very attractive, struggled with shyness that was supported by her weight problems. She had resolved to face them, and their circle of friends had encouraged her decision.

"Sounds great!" said Rebecca, "so long as it includes cheesecake. I've missed that."

"With chocolate sauce," said Brad.

"Yes. Everything is best with chocolate sauce." smiled Rebecca.

Saturday night, Rebecca squeezed into a little spandex number that didn't leave much to the imagination. It had hung on the back of her bedroom door as a goal in her effort. They arrived at Andy and Carol's house just after 8 pm. Several couples had already arrived and were enjoying the hot tub. Rebecca and Brad were soon slipping naked into the warm water.

As the evening progressed, more couples arrived. Finally, about eleven Carol and Andy called for the group's attention. Rebecca's achievement was recognized, and all present were able to view the results as Rebecca did her best imitation of a runway model.

Several of the ladies took Rebecca into another room for her surprise. The room was empty except for mattresses and pillows arranged around the edges. In the centre of the ceiling was an enormous hook. Hanging from it was a contraption of ropes and leather pieces. Rebecca was strapped into the harness so that she hung spread eagle facing the ceiling.

The straps of the harness supported her body at the upper back and buttocks, and she was surprisingly comfortable. Her wrists and ankles were secure, and she was unable to move.

The women worked with good-humoured chatter.

"We know how much you've missed your chocolate sauce, Becky," said Carol.

The warmed chocolate sauce was poured onto Rebecca's belly and spread all over her body. Chocolate dripped from her and onto drop cloths covering the carpet. The women laughed and rubbed chocolate covered hands on each other. Rebecca's eyes were blindfolded enabling her to enjoy a sensation of floating while the hands massaged her skin and orifices. The application of the chocolate was beginning to feel very good.

The men joined them shortly, and they hoisted her body higher into the air. The massaging hands were replaced with tongues lapping and exploring the underside of her body. It tickled and aroused her. The tongues moved with differing speeds and motions. Here and there a mouth sucked her skin. Electrical shocks of pleasure passed through her body making her nipples pucker, and her clit twitch with anticipation.

The harness was lowered slowly enabling the tongues to find her sides, shoulders, neck and hungry mouths to suckle her toes. The torment was incredible, and Rebecca whined for more. The tongues stopped, and she lay suspended in the air alone in her blindfolded darkness.

Then she felt fingers teasing the outer lips of her pussy. Her body was lowered again. The fingers exchanged for a tongue, which licked and lapped at the chocolate. Grazing her clit infrequently and sending flames to her brain with each flick.

Tongues found her right and then left breasts and did the same "can't-seem-to-find-the-spot" teasing of her nipples. Rebecca bucked and moaned.

More tongues found her belly, thighs, wrists fingers. Her body was on fire. The licking of her clit became more intense, and mouths found her nipples at last.

An object entered her vagina and moved slowly in and out. Rebecca's moans grew louder, and she began to beg to be fucked and fucked hard. One after another each man entered her pussy or covered his cock with chocolate and entered her mouth. At every moment she had two cocks in her thrusting and bringing her waves and waves of pleasure and release.

Rebecca shuddered with the last orgasm, and Brad removed the blindfold. All around her were groups of people enjoying her chocolate sauce and each other. Brad and Andy released Rebecca from the harness. Brad and Rebecca kissed.

"Now that was incentive," said Rebecca.

Andy and Brad took Rebecca back into the hot tub. Washing the stickiness off in the warm water, Andy and Brad placed Rebecca between them. Brad sucked each nipple in turn and Andy lapped and nibbled her neck. Rebecca was warm, relaxed and incredibly horny again. Andy slid his cock slowly into Rebecca's anus. Brad entered her pussy. There was pain and pleasure, biting and licking. Rebecca groaned with the double sensations. Andy and Brad thrust faster and the three moved together as the water washing over the edge of the hot tub. Rebecca's body shuddered with the force of the orgasm the rocked her and rose to roll over her again. Her nails dug into Brad's shoulders. Anne slid into the tub and began sucking Brad's nipples. John and Candy joined the group. Candy played with Rebecca's nipples and Andy's cock. John slid his cock into Anne. Soon, the others joined them and the hot tub became the focus of activity.

Rebecca and Brad wondered home at dawn, tired but very much in love.

Flight of Fantasy

Lesley had flown many times but never lost the thrill of air travel. She sat in the window seat, enjoying the lights of the city below.

The man beside her, dozing in the dim cabin light, smelled nice and was quite attractive. He had been preoccupied, and she hadn't had much of a conversation with him. He seemed to know the woman in the seat ahead of him.

The gentle rocking of an aircraft in flight always made Lesley horny. A long time graduate of the mile high club she was disappointed to have a less than co-operative seatmate on such a long flight. Lesley shifted in her seat and scanned the immediate area for any likely prospects. The woman ahead of her seatmate was seated alone, and the people behind were a geriatric couple together. Her sexual frustration increased by the second. The lights were down, and most of the passengers were asleep.

She let her hand slide along her seatmate's thigh, and her fingers playfully caressed his zipper. There was no response. She rummaged in her purse for her travel toothbrush tube. Then, she positioned herself in the seat raising one knee and wedging it against the empty seat in front of her. She pulled her skirt up exposing her smooth shaven pussy. Undoing the front of her top, she freed both breasts and began to play with the nipples. She pinched and teased her nipples to attention and bending slightly forward was able to lick her nipples in turn. Her fingers parted the lips of her moist aching pussy, and she massaged her clit with a circular motion. Lesley took the toothbrush tube and slid the tip of it into her vagina.

Her seatmate startled her by moving to take one of her nipples into his mouth and sucking it. Just then, the seat ahead of him tipped back allowing its occupant to slide an arm through. She grabbed the tube and pumped Lesley's hungry hole with it. Lesley's massaged her clit rapidly. Lesley's breathing was heavy, and the tube made squishing sounds as it brought her increasing pleasure.

The seat ahead of her came forward causing her to slide down in her seat and spread her legs wider. The woman was able to get a finger in Lesley's anus and thrust deeper with the tube. The man's mouth moved back and forth between Lesley's pert nipples.

Passion crashed over her and rose again to crash much harder. A long practiced silence in such situations was completely lost for Lesley. She moaned loudly, and he had to cover her mouth.

Suddenly the impending arrival of the plane to its destination was announced. She struggled to dress and gather up her things as the lights came on. She followed the other passengers out of the plane.

The woman was ahead of her, and the man was behind her. She felt his hand under her skirt caressing her butt and attempting at every possible moment to slide into her like a wetness-seeking missile. She leaned forward to permit his access when the queue of passengers slowed. She was dizzy with the torment of the interrupted contacts. As they walked quickly along the airport hallway towards the customs area, he grabbed her elbow and said

"Airport Security, Ma'am. You'll have to come with me."

He directed her to a staff area where there was a counter for reviewing luggage. No staff persons were in sight. The woman had followed them.

"I'm sorry, but we'll have to search you for weapons." She said.

Lesley's clothes were removed and placed neatly on a shelf. The woman caressed her and sucked on one breast while the man sucked the other. She was pushed back onto the counter and her legs spread. The counter was quite cold and heightened her sensitivities. The woman undressed and placed her nipples in Lesley's mouth. The man began licking her inner thighs. His thumb massaged her clit while his fingers pumped her drooling hole. They turned her over, and the woman slid underneath her.

Lesley licked the outer lips of the woman's pussy and then darted her tongue inside. The woman massaged her own breasts and ground her hips into Lesley's face. The man licked Lesley's ass cheeks and then thrust his fingers into her pussy and anus at the same time. Then he thrust his cock deeply and roughly into her. She bucked and moaned forgetting the woman for a moment. She wanted to be impaled on his enormous cock. The woman grabbed her hair and pulled her head down and back into position.

Stopping just on the edge of orgasm, the man waited for the woman to cum with Lesley's tongue moving rapidly in sync with her fingers which pumped inside the woman. The man moved slowly inside of Lesley torturing her with desire.

Finally, he thrust harder and faster, and they both came with shudders and moans.

Quickly they gathered themselves together and hustled down the corridor to the arrivals lobby. They were each greeted by awaiting family and did not speak or acknowledge each other again. The ebbing tide of the airport visitors separated them and pulled them into the morning light.

Under the Skull and Cross Bones

She ignored the wind that pulled at her hair and clothing as if trying to complete her disrobing. She shifted her weight slightly and stretched her upraised leg before bracing her foot back against the aft deck railing. The coolness of the open air excited and awakened her exposed skin. Her nipples stood out to greet the chill. She gripped the tiller firmer as her body trembled in response to the man's tongue.

There wasn't much moonlight, but the stars were bright. The night was quiet save for the lapping of the waves against the hull of the ship. The ship gently pitched and rocked as she watched the stars and the movement of the sails closely.

The man's head bobbed steadily between her body and the aft deck railing. His tongue was lapping in rapid circles while his fingers pumped her sheathe as no man-sword had ever done. Her back arched and her grip tightened on the tiller as the tide of pleasure rolled in.

Shortly, the man rose to his feet tasting her exposed flesh as he did. She guided his mouth to her nipples with one hand while maintaining her grip on the tiller with the other. The man kissed her full on the mouth hungrily. His tongue snaked into her throat.

"Unsheathe your sword, man! Ye waste the night!" She growled.

Swiftly, the man was inside her, pumping and pounding her against the side of the ship. She moaned and cried out in the passion of the moment but never once let go of the tiller. When they were done the deed, she pushed him away and rearranged her clothing.

"Resume yer post, sailor. Hold fast the course."

"Aye, Aye, Captain." said the man, while she took one last look around the deck and retired to her cabin.

"SHIP AHOY!!" was the cry just before dawn.

Captain Deborah tumbled out of bed and into her breaches, fastening her sword holster about her hips as she raced up the stairs to the bridge.

An English frigate was approaching to starboard with only a handful of crew on deck.

"AHOY, the Merry Wench!" bellowed a voice from the approaching vessel.

"AHOY! Where be yer Captain?!" responded Deborah's First Mate.

"Most of the crew took sick and died. There's only a few of us left."

"Have ye the plague, then?"

"No! 'Twas the grub at the last Port. Not enough maggots in the pork!"

A chorus of laughter followed making it clear that the remaining crew were heavy into the grog.

Deborah caught sight of some females trussed to the main mast. They looked healthy enough, so she and a few of her crew boarded the Lady Anne.

They discovered six crewmembers and as many women on the deck. Below deck was a huge cargo of stores including wine, dried goods, livestock, and fine fabrics. Locked in another area were a few dozen more women. There were a large number of trunks containing the personal items of these women.

Upon questioning the women, Deborah discovered that they were brides-to-be destined for settlers in New England. The women had not been tended since the death of the ship's Captain and had been terrorized by the drunken lot that remained on board.

The Captain ordered her First Mate and selected crew members to sail the Lady Anne in pursuit of the Merry Wench and returned to her vessel.

The Merry Wench resumed her course for the uncharted island homeport of Captain Deborah and her crew with the Lady Anne following. By nightfall, they were anchored in its sheltered harbour, and much of the booty of the Lady Anne had been brought ashore.

The women had been made to help unload the ship and in exchange had been permitted to retain ownership of their trunks for the time being. The women arranged themselves in a sheltered area just on the edge of the jungle. Skirts and dresses hung form vine clotheslines, and women wandered about in chemises still damp from wading into shore.

Deborah had her crew build a huge bonfire, and they roasted boars, which were prolific on the island and a favourite meal of the crew. Grog flowed freely, and all was pleasant. The women were afraid but relieved to be on dry land and becoming somewhat resigned to their fate as prisoners of the infamous pirate Captain Deborah Flint and her bloodthirsty crew.

Deborah had all the women lined up for her inspection. She enjoyed making each one display her value to the crew. Deborah stripped them, exposed their breasts to the tip of her whip and their bared buttocks to the lash of it if they denied her merriment.

The Captain allowed her men to make their choices, settling any disputes with an arm wrestle and they set about educating the young women on the arts of pleasing a pirate.

Deborah was left with seven women unclaimed.

She made the women walk single file into the jungle along a well-worn path. It was dark and difficult to see despite the torch that Deborah carried. Two of the women stumbled causing Deborah to crack her whip and bark orders.

 The women, ashamed of their nakedness and terrified of their plight began to whimper and cry as they made their way through the bush.

Finally, they arrived at a waterfall and hot springs in a large clearing. The women entered the hot springs pool without the need of much encouragement.

Deborah told them that while they would find the water soothing, they would taste the bite of her whip sharply if they did not do exactly as instructed.

Deborah climbed up on a rock and disrobed while barking out orders like rapid gunfire. She punctuated her remarks with cracks of her whip.

The women massaged and stroked each other as instructed. Each woman kissed the next one. Hands moved under the water kneading tired flesh and tenderly easing aches and pains. The women divided into pairs and the seventh woman was paired with Deborah much to her obvious terror.

Each pair kissed deeply, tongues touching tentatively at first and then more aggressively. Hands that massaged began to caress, and mouths found hardened nipples. Embarrassed giggles turned to moans of pleasure.

One woman of each pair sat upon the rock edge and spread her legs wide for her partner. Deborah painstakingly instructed the women still in the water on the art of pleasing themselves and another woman.

Tongues flicked with delicious torment introducing purity to the decadence of focused pleasure. The women on the rock edge moaned and wriggled with repeated waves of bliss. Then, the sources of this new delight were rewarded with the insistent lapping of their partner's tongues. Satisfaction was found, lost and reclaimed over and over again and yet remained elusive. The women hungered for more and all begged for the experienced tongue of Captain Deborah.

Deborah climbed out of the hot springs pool and reclined at the edge of the clearing on a cushion of ferns and moss. The women gathered around her in a circle, breast positioned for her to suckle. She tasted each pair in turn and encouraged them to continue with their neighbours.

Exhausted she lay back on the moss and closed her eyes. She felt seven mouths on her body almost immediately. Two mouths licked between her legs taking turns tormenting her secret button. Mouths were sucking her nipples, and someone was sucking the toes of each foot. There was a sheath of sweetness positioned over her face, and she lapped at it ravenously.

Deborah's body shuddered as a tidal wave of passion crashed over her and rose again. The women moved together as a crew intent on riding an insatiable monsoon of desire. It began to rain, but no one noticed.

A WINTER EVE

Tap upon my window
And swiftly enter in,
I await your coming
With the warmth of love and wine.
I will put aside your cloak
And brush away the snow
And kiss the chill
And thunder
From the memories
Of your soul
The softness of my skin
So gentle is your touch
Take me in your arms
And love me till the dawn.
I tremble as I ponder
So eagerly I wait.
So, tap upon my window
And swiftly enter in.